Barry the Burglar's
LAST JOB

Richard Tulloch

Barry the Burglar's LAST JOB

Illustrated by Coral Tulloch

Omnibus
DIPPER

Scholastic Publications Ltd,
Villiers House,
Clarendon Avenue,
Leamington Spa,
Warks CV32 6EB, UK

Scholastic Inc.,
730 Broadway, New York, NY 10003, USA

Ashton Scholastic Pty Ltd,
PO Box 579, Gosford, New South Wales,
Australia

Ashton Scholastic Ltd,
Private Bag 1, Penrose, Auckland,
New Zealand

First published by Omnibus Books, part of the
Ashton Scholastic Group, 1992
Reprinted 1993
This edition, only available as part of Scholastic Literacy Centre:
Get Reading! (Blue Set), first published in the UK by Scholastic
Publications Ltd, 1994

Text copyright © Richard Tulloch 1992
Illustrations copyright © Coral Tulloch 1992

ISBN 0 590 53352 5

Omnibus Dipper is a registered trademark of Ashton Scholastic
Pty Ltd

All rights reserved

Printed by Cox & Wyman Ltd, Reading, Berks

10 9 8 7 6 5 4 3

This book is sold subject to the condition that it shall not, by way
of trade or otherwise, be lent, resold, hired out, or otherwise
circulated without the publisher's prior consent in any form of
binding or cover other than that in which it is published and
without a similar condition, including this condition, being
imposed upon the subsequent purchaser.

Illustrator's dedication

For Maxine Clark

Barry was the best, the boldest and the brainiest burglar in the whole town.

No wall was too thick, no lock too tricky and no watchman too watchful to keep Burglar Barry out. He could get in anywhere and burgle anything he wanted.

And he had never been caught.

Burglar Barry's home was a warehouse—
a great big shed with a great big padlock on
the door.

The warehouse was empty and dusty. At one end was a grimy table and chair at which Barry ate his dinner and at the other end was a dirty old mattress which he used for a bed.

But under the dusty floorboards Barry kept his Loot—the money, jewels and other treasures he collected from his burgling expeditions.

One Monday night, when the whole town slept and the moon hid behind clouds, Burglar Barry robbed the Baker Street Bank.

He'd passed the bank that afternoon just as the bank manager was shutting up for the night, switching on the burglar alarm and locking the front door behind him. But Barry saw that the manager had left the safe door open.

"How stupid some people are!" thought Barry. "Fancy a bank leaving a safe door open! It's asking for trouble!"

So as the town hall clock struck midnight, Burglar Barry, with his sack on his back, a glint in his eyes and a pounding in his heart, crept through the streets in his soft-soled sneakers which sounded not a whisper when they touched the ground.

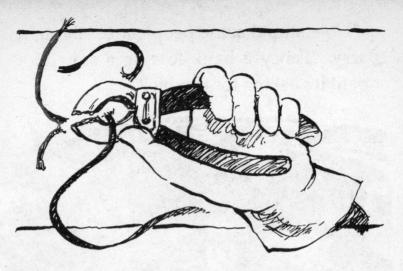

Round to the back door of the bank he crept. He snipped the wires of the burglar alarm with his burglar's snippers, picked the lock with a burglar's bent hairpin, glided through the bank to the open safe, loaded the money into his sack and got clean away.

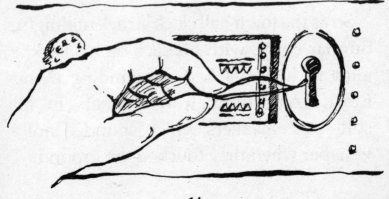

That night Barry had twenty-three thousand, four hundred and sixty pounds and seventy-nine pence to hide under the dusty floorboards of his burglar's warehouse.

Café Burglar

Next morning the headline in the paper read DARING BANK JOB, and Barry smiled a secret smile.

At the bottom corner of page five of the paper he found another interesting news item:

FAMOUS ART EXHIBITION COMES TO THE GRIFFIN GALLERY.

"How stupid some people are!" thought Barry. "Fancy a gallery telling everyone they've got all that valuable art coming in. It's asking for trouble!"

So on Tuesday night, as the town hall clock struck one in the morning, Burglar Barry, with his sack on his back, a glint in his eyes and a pounding in his heart, crept through the streets in his soft-soled sneakers which sounded not a whisper when they touched the ground.

He shinned up a drainpipe to an upstairs window of the Griffin Gallery, prised it open with his burglar's crowbar, hid in the ladies toilet while the security guard went past, filled his sack with priceless works of art and got clean away.

Barry hid the Loot under the dusty floor-boards of his warehouse. He had three paintings of ladies with no clothes on, a china vase from the tomb of an ancient pharaoh and a statue made of a sort of metal ... um ... of a, well, a wheel thing which was sort of ... well, to tell the truth, neither Barry nor anyone else had ever worked out *what* it was a statue of, but he'd read in the paper that it was worth a lot of money so he thought he ought to steal it.

Next day the headline in the morning paper read GANG OUTWITS GALLERY GUARDS, and Barry smiled a secret smile.

At the bottom corner of page sixteen of the paper, he saw an advertisement:

CARETAKER WANTED

APPLY ROSEMOUNT MANSIONS

"How stupid some people are," thought Barry. "Fancy putting an ad in the paper to tell everyone there's no caretaker on duty at a mansion house! It's asking for trouble."

So on Wednesday night, as the town hall clock struck two, Burglar Barry, with his sack on his back, a glint in his eyes and a pounding in his heart, crept through the streets in his soft-soled sneakers which sounded not a whisper when they touched the ground.

Burgling Rosemount Mansions was easy.

Barry was over the ivy-covered wall in no time flat. He padded up the driveway towards the house, which loomed at him out of the darkness. The front door wasn't even locked.

"No wonder they need a caretaker," muttered Barry. "A junior burglar just out of reform school could burgle this place with no trouble at all."

It was dark inside the house, but that was no problem for Barry. He crept in and out of the rooms, feeling his way around the walls and mantelpieces, picking up a piece of china here, a little painting there, a statuette and some silverware. Hanging behind a door was a heavy velvet dress encrusted with diamonds around the collar.

In less than ten minutes his sack was full
and he'd got clean away.

Down the path, over the wall, back through the town and into the safety of his dusty warehouse crept Burglar Barry.

Then he opened his sack and examined the Loot.

It wasn't what he expected.

The valuable china turned out to be a cracked teapot and seven cups from three different teasets.

The heavy velvet dress was only an old dressing-gown with a torn pocket, and its diamonds weren't really diamonds—only a few dried cornflakes from where someone had spilt breakfast on the collar.

The picture was a fingerpainting labelled *To Gran. Happy Birthday, Love Sharon.*

Barry gnashed his teeth and swore the worst swearword he could think of (which was far too bad to go into this story). Then he slumped down on his dirty mattress and lay awake all night wondering what could have gone wrong.

Next day the headline in the morning paper read, SCUMBAG BURGLAR! WHAT SORT OF ANIMAL WOULD DO THIS?

And as Barry read on, he didn't smile a secret smile.

"The thief who broke into the old people's home at Rosemount Mansions must be the lowest form of life," he read.

"Family heirlooms, presents from grand-children and other items of sentimental value were stolen last night. Mrs Beatrice Morgan, who lost a painting given to her for her eightieth birthday by her grand-daughter Sharon, was in tears. Mr Gordon Trumble lost his dressing-gown. Miss Iris O'Hara had her favourite teapot stolen. 'There was nothing special about it,' she said, 'but tea made in other pots just doesn't taste the same.' "

Burglar Barry swallowed hard. Robbing banks and art galleries was one thing. But this was different.

On Thursday night, as the town hall clock struck three, Burglar Barry, with his sack on his back, a glint in his eyes and a pounding in his heart, climbed over the ivy-covered wall and padded down the path towards the front door of Rosemount Mansions. It was locked.

Barry tossed his burglar's rope up on to the roof of Rosemount Mansions, shinned up to the skylight, prised it open with his burglar's crowbar, slipped through into the attic and paused for a moment, listening in the dark.

The house was utterly quiet.

Barry crept down the stairs to the living-room.

"Poor defenceless old people," he thought. "Well, they're in for a big surprise!"

He was just bending down to open his burglar's sack when he received a big surprise himself.

Bang! went a blow to the back of Barry's head.

"*Ooof!*" went Barry.

Whoosh! went a rope under Barry's feet, catching him round the ankles and sweeping him feet first up into the air.

"*Urgghh! Help!*" went Barry.

Click! went the light switch, flooding the living-room with light. And there were Mrs Beatrice Morgan carrying a rolling pin, Mr Gordon Trumble brandishing a heavy walking stick and all the other defenceless old people armed to the teeth with carving knives and shifting spanners, golf clubs and cricket bats and broom handles. Miss Iris O'Hara threatened him with the pointy end of a pink umbrella.

"We got him!" shouted the defenceless old people all at once.

For the first time in his life, Burglar Barry, the best, the boldest and the brainiest burglar in town, was caught!

"Now, young man," said Miss Iris O'Hara, pointing the pink umbrella at Barry's belly button, "perhaps you could tell us what you mean by breaking into our house in the dead of night."

"Look!" said Mrs Morgan. "He's got Sharon's painting in his bag."

"And my dressing-gown," said Mr Gordon Trumble.

"And my favourite china teapot," said Miss Iris O'Hara. "This is no ordinary burglar we've caught here. This is the Scumbag Burglar!"

"How stupid some people are," said Mr Gordon Trumble, tapping his walking stick on Barry's ribs. "Fancy trying to burgle the same house two nights in a row! It's asking for trouble! Well, we're not so defenceless as you might think, Mr Scumbag!"

"B-b-b-but-but-but," stammered Barry, "I'm not a scumbag. I'm a good burglar. I came here to return all your things."

"A likely story!" scoffed Mrs Beatrice Morgan.

"I don't rob defenceless old people," said Barry. "B-b-banks and art galleries—that's the sort of work I do."

"So you're a bank robber, eh?" said Mr Gordon Trumble. "Well, my son was the manager of the Baker Street Bank. When it was burgled on Monday he lost his job!"

"Art galleries, eh?" said Miss Iris O'Hara. "My daughter is a sculptor and her best statue was in the Griffin Gallery. It's a sort of metal wheel thing and it's very, very good. But last Tuesday a burglar stole it and no one will ever see it again."

They watched Barry's face very carefully as they said these things. And by the way his eyes flickered from side to side they knew, and Barry knew they knew, and they knew Barry knew they knew, that he was the thief they were talking about.

So for the rest of the night he had to behave himself.

As the town hall clock struck four in the morning Burglar Barry switched on the dingy light and Mrs Beatrice Morgan, Mr Gordon Trumble, Miss Iris O'Hara and all the other defenceless old people peered into the gloom of his burglar's warehouse.

"What an awful, dusty, dirty place!" exclaimed Miss Iris O'Hara. "I thought burglars lived in seaside mansions on the fruits of their ill-gotten gains."

"Some burglars do," growled Barry. "Some burglars are so stupid they let everyone know how rich they are, and then they get caught."

Mrs Beatrice Morgan looked at the grimy table and chair and the dirty mattress. "All the same, this must be such a lonely place to live!" she said.

Barry said nothing. He just bit his bottom
lip, and wiped the back of his hand across
his eyes. Then he pulled up the floorboards
and started loading Loot into his sack.

It was quiet at four-thirty in the morning, because the town hall clock didn't bother to strike half hours. Burglar Barry crept down the silent streets in his soft-soled sneakers.

At the bank, Miss Iris O'Hara kept watch and Mrs Beatrice Morgan lent Barry a hair-pin to pick the lock so he could put the money back into the safe.

At the Griffin Gallery Mr Gordon Trumble gave him a leg up so that he could climb in through a top window and hang the paintings back on the walls.

Barry couldn't remember which way up the funny sort of wheel statue had been, but he hoped no one would notice if he put it back upside-down.

Then the defenceless old people marched Barry back to the front door of Rosemount Mansions.

"Now, Burglar Barry," said Mrs Beatrice Morgan, "we want you to promise to give up burgling and go straight for ever."

"I don't think I can," said Barry. "Burgling's been my life for so long, it's the only job I'm really good at."

"Why don't you become our caretaker?" said Miss Iris O'Hara. "You could come and live in the cosy downstairs caretaker's flat. And you know all the tricks that other burglars use and you'd be really good at keeping them out."

Barry thought of the dusty warehouse which had been his lonely home for as long as he could remember. And he looked around at the shining faces of all the defenceless old people. And he wondered what it would be like to live in a cosy caretaker's flat with friends around to keep him company.

Barry smiled a secret smile. But this time he smiled it out loud.

"I'd like that," he said. "Thank you."

"Hooray," cheered everybody.

Whoosh! went the wind.

Slam! went the front door of Rosemount Mansions.

"Oh no, we're locked out!" said Mr Gordon Trumble.

"Oh no, we're not," said Caretaker Barry.

And with a glint in his eyes and a pounding in his heart, he unwound his burglar's rope for one last job.

Robert Swindells

"Faithful, fearless, full of fun,
Winter, summer, rain or sun,
One for five, and five for one –
THE OUTFIT!"

*Meet The Outfit—Jillo, Titch, Mickey and Shaz. Share in
their adventures as they fearlessly investigate any mystery,
and injustice, that comes their way . . .*

Move over, Famous Five, The Outfit are here!

The Secret of Weeping Wood

The Outfit are determined to discover the truth about the
eerie crying, coming from scary Weeping Wood. Is the
wood really haunted?

We Didn't Mean To, Honest!

The marriage of creepy Kenneth Kilchaffinch to snooty
Prunella could mean that Froglet Pond, and all its
wildlife, will be destroyed. So it's up to The Outfit to
make sure the marriage is off . . . But how?

Kidnap at Denton Farm

Farmer Denton's new wind turbine causes a protest
meeting in Lenton, and The Outfit find themselves in
the thick of it. But a *kidnap* is something they didn't
bargain for . . .

The Ghosts of Givenham Keep

What is going on at spooky Givenham Keep? It can't be
haunted, can it? The Outfit are just about to find out . . .

BABYSITTERS LITTLE SISTER

Meet Karen Brewer. She's seven years old and her big sister Kristy runs the Babysitters Club. And Karen's always having adventures of her own . . . Read all about her in her very own series.

YOUNG HIPPO MAGIC

Magic is in the air with these enchanting stories
from Young Hippo Magic – stories about ordinary,
everyday children who discover that in the world of
magic, anything is possible!

The Little Pet Dragon
Philippa Gregory

James is thrilled when he finds a tiny greyhound
puppy! But aren't those scales on its body? And
isn't that snouty face rather dragon-like? James
doesn't notice, because his puppy is glimmering
with a very strong magic . . .

My Friend's a Gris-Quok
Malorie Blackman

A Young Hippo Magic story for early readers

Alex has a deep, dark secret. He's half Gris-Quok,
which is fantastic, because he can turn himself into
anything he likes! However, he can only do it *three*
times a day . . .

The Marmalade Pony
Linda Newbery

A Young Hippo Magic story for early readers

Hannah has always longed for a pony of her very
own, but the best she can do is imagine. Then one
day her dad starts making something mysterious in
the shed . . .

YOUNG HiPPO SPOOKY

Do you like to be spooked? Do you dare to be *scared?* If you're *really* brave, then get stuck into these deliciously spooky but funny ghost stories from Young Hippo Spooky!

Scarem's House
Malcolm Yorke

When the ghostly house belonging to Scarem O'Gool and his family is invaded by humans, there's only one solution. The O'Gools are going to have to *haunt* them out!

The Screaming Demon Ghostie
Jean Chapman

A Young Hippo Spooky story for early readers

Kate Kelly doesn't believe there's any such thing as the Screaming Demon Ghostie of the old forest track. And one dark night, she sets off to prove it!